The Montgomery Street Gang

Emily C. Ramsdell
Illustrated by James R. Chrisfield

ISBN 978-1-63814-732-9 (Paperback)
ISBN 978-1-63814-734-3 (Hardcover)
ISBN 978-1-63814-733-6 (Digital)

Covenant Books, Inc.
11661 Hwy 707
Murrells Inlet, SC 29576
www.covenantbooks.com

To my husband, Jim, to whose encouragements
the writing of this book owes so much.

To our two precious grandsons, Trey Ramsdell and Logan Ramsdell

Trust in the Lord with all your heart and do not lean on your own
understanding. In all your ways acknowledge Him,
and He will direct your paths. (Proverbs 3:5–6)

—ER

For my grandchildren,
Emmeline, Hadley, Ruby, and Everett

—JC

Chapter 1

It was a cold December day. It was snowing, and the wind was beating against the faces of the five kids walking down Montgomery Street. To everyone in the neighborhood, these kids were well-known as the Montgomery Street Gang.

There was Tony, and he was tough. The kids called him Big T—*T* for trouble! He yelled a lot, and maybe that's why he was the ringleader of the group. Then there was Big T's younger brother, Dashawn, who did everything his brother told him to do. Next in the gang was Butch. He was big for his age and really mean. Diego was the neighborhood bully. Tagging along behind the gang was Maria. The guys really didn't want her following them. Maria's mother died, and she came to live with Big T's family until they could find a home for her. Maria always had with her the one possession that meant the most to her, an old raggedy doll.

Usually, the Montgomery Street Gang did not go to school. Instead, they spent some of their time at their makeshift hideout or gang headquarters at the end of Montgomery Street, just past the open field in an abandoned garage. Wherever the Montgomery Street Gang went, there was trouble! They beat up on kids, destroyed other people's property, lied, cheated, and stole things from the corner drugstore. They made life miserable for those living on Montgomery Street.

The people who lived on Montgomery Street were all colors, shapes, and sizes. On the street stood a lot of vacant houses, some boarded up, and others needed a lot of work. Homes that at one time were beautiful were now in rough shape. Broken down garages and empty storefronts covered with graffiti dotted the landscape. In the remaining houses lived the neighborhood kids of Montgomery Street, most of whom roamed the streets to escape the boredom and loneliness. But in the midst of all this brokenness on Montgomery Street, there stood an old brick building.

Chapter 2

*T*he old brick building was the home of the Christian Community Center. For many of the kids, the center was a place of refuge, a place where they felt accepted for who they were. Mr. Steve and his wife, Ms. Michele, directed the program at the center along with their staff. The neighborhood kids loved going to the center. They felt safe there. At the center, they were treated with love and respect. For the neighborhood kids, the center was the best part of their day. At the end of the school day, the center kids ran as fast as they could to go to the center, hoping to avoid meeting up with the Montgomery Street Gang. The Montgomery Street Gang was familiar with the center too. Just the night before, they had great fun smashing in some of the windows of the center. Mr. Steve and the center staff had a pretty good idea who was behind the vandalism at the center the night before, so they started to pray for the Montgomery Street Gang.

Now the center boys' favorite time was being with Mr. Steve, who always had plenty of games planned for them. But as usual, their most favorite time was in the gym playing basketball, shooting hoops at rims that actually had nets.

You could hear the girls with Ms. Michele. She always had some arts and crafts set up at the tables. Many of the girls just wanted to spend time hair braiding and polishing their nails. Homework? Well, some diligent kids would work on their homework, but for the most part, it was just a time to be a kid! Life was hard for most of these kids, but the center was a place of safety. After games, activities, and snacks, Mr. Steve and Ms. Michele had all the kids gather around for Bible time.

Since it was December, the center kids were planning and practicing for their upcoming Christmas pageant. Meanwhile, as the wind blew especially hard, the gang headed down Montgomery Street to their hideout. But just like every other day, they passed by the Christian Community Center.

Butch muttered something about the kids going to the center to a Bible club.

"They read stories from the Bible! Just a place for wimps!" he said.

Dashawn added, "They learn about God. I wonder who God is?"

As they walked by the Christian Community Center, they noticed a sign that read Christmas Pageant Rehearsal Today.

"Hmmm," said Big T. "Christmas pageant… I wonder what that is?"

Diego said, "Hey, maybe they've got food. Let's go in and see what's going on."

It was snowing hard now as the wind continued to blow, so it didn't take much convincing for the gang to make up their minds to go in. And in they went—Big T, Dashawn, Butch, Diego, and Maria, holding on tightly to her raggedy doll.

They went in making so much noise that everyone in the Christian Community Center turned around to see what the commotion was about. When the center kids looked up, they whispered among themselves, "Oh no, it's the Montgomery Street Gang!"

Just at that moment, Mr. Steve smiled and greeted the newcomers and invited them to come in. It sure felt warm inside the center, so the gang made their way in and marched down to the front row and sat down.

Big T spoke up, "We wanna know about this Christmas pageant. What's a Christmas pageant?"

Chapter 3

$\mathcal{M}$s. Michele replied, "It's like a play—a Christmas play."

Butch interrupted, "Oh, you mean like Santa Claus, elves, and reindeer?"

"Oh, no," Ms. Michele said. "I'm talking about the *real* Christmas story, the one from the Bible."

The gang looked at one another with puzzled looks.

Ms. Michele continued, "The Christmas story about Mary, Joseph, the baby Jesus, the shepherds, the angels—"

Just then, Butch interrupted, "Angels! *We* can be the 'angels'!" And the four boys laughed!

Maria spoke up, "Lady, who's Mary and Joseph? And who is baby Jesus?"

Ms. Michele looked for a moment at the frail girl who had asked that question, and she realized that Maria was serious. She didn't know anything at all about Joseph, Mary, and the baby Jesus.

Ms. Michele told all the children to sit down, then picking up her Bible, she said, "This is God's special book that tells us all about the very first Christmas. Would you like to hear about it?"

The children all nodded. The Montgomery Street Gang just sat there.

Ms. Michele began. "One night, long ago, God, the one who made the world, sent His very own Son from heaven to earth to be born in a manger in the little village of Bethlehem. The mother of this baby was Mary. She had come to Bethlehem with her husband, Joseph, from their home in Nazareth. Bethlehem was crowded with travelers. Joseph and Mary could not find a place to stay except in a stable, a place where animals were kept. God had chosen this place for His Son, Jesus, to be born.

"Before Mary laid the baby Jesus in the manger, which is a feedbox for animals, she wrapped Him in a long strip of cloth. Even as she was perhaps singing His first lullaby, a group of shepherds was out on the hillside, watching their sheep. Suddenly, they saw a great light and an angel. The angel said, 'Fear not, for behold, I bring you good news of great joy. For unto you is born this day in the city of David, a Savior, which is Christ the Lord. And this shall be a sign unto you, you will find the baby wrapped in swaddling cloth lying in a manger.'

"As the shepherds watched in amazement, they saw many, many angels appear. The angels praised God, saying, 'Glory to God in the highest and on earth peace, goodwill toward men.' The shepherds hurried to Bethlehem. They searched and found Mary and Joseph and the baby. The baby was lying in a manger, just like the angel said. Mary may have held the baby Jesus for the shepherds to see. This baby was different from all other babies—He was the Son of God!"

Everything and everyone in the Christian Community Center was quiet. Big T broke the silence. "Is this story for real?"

Chapter 4

$\mathcal{M}$s. Michele nodded her head. "Yes."

Big T said, "If this story is real, why did God send His Son to this earth?"

A couple of the Bible club kids had that look on their face like, *What a dumb question*, but Ms. Michele responded quickly, "That's a good question."

She opened her Bible again. "God sent His Son to earth because He loves you. It says so right here in the Bible (Jer. 31:33). God loves you with an everlasting love. Just think, the Creator of this world loves *you and me*, and He wants us to be in heaven with Him someday. But there is one thing that separates all of us from God, and that is sin."

Diego interrupted, "What's sin?"

Ms. Michele continued, "Sin is anything you think, say, or do that displeases God, like lying, cheating, having a bad attitude, and destroying someone else's property."

Just then, one of the Bible club kids interrupted, "Mr. Steve, tell them about Jesus and what He came to do about our sin."

Mr. Steve grabbed his Bible and he began. "The Lord Jesus, God's perfect Son, came to this earth as a baby. He grew up, and when He became a man, He willingly allowed wicked men to nail Him to a cross. And when those nails went into His hands and feet, what came out? Yes, blood. He gave His life's blood in payment for your sin and mine. What a price to pay! The Lord Jesus died and was buried, but three days later, He came alive again. And because He lives, He has the power to forgive your sin and mine."

The members of the gang squirmed in their seats. They knew they had done wrong things, and now they knew what the Bible had to say about that. Big T was the first to move, and motioning to the other gang members, they got up and walked out. Mr. Steve followed them to the door, inviting them to come back another day. In the meantime, the center kids started to get ready for the Christmas pageant rehearsal. The next afternoon, the center kids were shocked.

Chapter 5

*J*ust as Ms. Michele was starting Bible club, in walked the Montgomery Street Gang—Big T, Dashawn, Butch, and Diego, followed by Maria with her raggedy doll. You could just feel the tension between the gang members and the center kids. You could almost read the minds of the center kids, thoughts like, *I wish they weren't here.*

THOUGHT
for
THE DAY

EPHESIANS   CHAPTER 4
4:32.
BE KIND TO ONE ANOTHER,
TENDERHEARTED,
FORGIVING ONE ANOTHER,
AS GOD IN CHRIST
HAS FORGIVEN
YOU.

Immediately, Mr. Steve got up and welcomed everyone. He opened his Bible and read these words, "Be kind to one another, tenderhearted, forgiving one another, as God in Christ has forgiven you" (Eph. 4:32).

The center kids were now the ones who were squirming. They knew not showing love and forgiveness was their sin. It was something they needed to confess or tell on themselves to God. Mr. Steve, Ms. Michele, and the staff were now praying not only for the Montgomery Street Gang but also for the center kids.

Day after day, the members of the gang came to the center. Day after day, they heard about God's love and forgiveness. The center kids began to show that love and forgiveness to the Montgomery Street Gang. Maria became a favorite at the center. When the center staff found out about Maria needing a place to stay—a home—they all started praying for her, even the center kids.

December days on Montgomery Street continued cold, with heavy snow and lots of wind. It was getting closer to Christmas. The center was such a warm place to be sheltered from the winter cold, and the center was decorated for the holidays: lights, music, and something a lot of the kids didn't have, a Christmas tree. Every afternoon, the center kids and members of the gang came together, and after some delicious Christmas cookies and hot chocolate, they continued their pageant rehearsals. But this particular day, some different things happened.

Chapter 6

As soon as the Montgomery Street Gang arrived at the center, Big T asked Mr. Steve if he could speak with him. Big T told Mr. Steve that the gang was responsible for the damage to the center's windows. He said he was sorry, and he asked Mr. Steve to forgive him. Mr. Steve knew this was an answer to their prayers.

When Big T and Mr. Steve joined the rest of the group, Ms. Michele was just finishing up Bible club time. She looked at her watch. "Oh," she said. "We must get to our Christmas pageant rehearsal. There's not a lot of time left." The kids scurried around getting into their costumes and getting scenery in place.

All of a sudden, someone shouted, "We don't have a baby Jesus."

Sure enough, the manger was empty. Ms. Michele said, "Surely we must have a doll around here we can use."

Everyone started searching. At about that time, the gang looked over at Maria, but Maria was gone. Where was Maria? There was Maria. She was kneeling at the manger.

Ms. Michele came over to her. Maria said, "I would like my doll to be the baby Jesus," and she lovingly placed her raggedy doll in the manger.

Ms. Michele thanked Maria and then said, "Maria, would you like to know the real Jesus as your Savior?"

Maria nodded. Ms. Michele shared with Maria how she could pray and talk with God and ask Jesus to forgive her sin and be her Savior. Once again, Maria knelt in front of the manger. She prayed and asked the Lord Jesus to come into her life, forgive her sin, and be her Savior.

As Ms. Michele and Maria got up to leave, everyone was surprised to see Big T, Dashawn, and Diego kneeling at the manger, making a decision to accept Christ as their Savior. Mr. Steve went and sat near Butch, talking with him briefly, but Butch said he was not ready to make a decision. Mr. Steve whispered, "I will be praying for you."

Some of the Montgomery Street Gang not only were becoming a part of the center family but, more importantly, a part of God's family!

There were only a few more days before the Christmas pageant. Everyone was getting excited, even members of the gang. But this day, when they arrived at the center, Maria was not with them.

Chapter 7

At the center, Big T told everyone the social worker was coming that afternoon to take Maria away. Everyone felt sad. Someone said, "We need to pray for her."

When the time of prayer was over, the center staff was there to help with the last rehearsal before the pageant that night.

Maria was at Big T's house, sitting at the edge of what used to be a couch that served as her bed. Tears were running down her face. Looking out the window, she watched the snow falling hard. It was only two days before Christmas. Maria knew she had to leave, but she didn't know where she was going this time. She never felt so alone. Suddenly, she remembered a Bible verse Ms. Michele taught her on her fingers, "Jesus will never leave me." She kept saying those words over and over. She knew God would take care of her.

In another room, Maria heard voices. The door to the room opened, and there stood Mr. Steve and his wife, Ms. Michele. Behind them stood the social worker.

Tears ran down Maria's face. She didn't want to say goodbye to her center teachers. Mr. Steve had a smile on his face.

Ms. Michele spoke to Maria, "How would you like to come and live with us?"

Maria couldn't believe the words she was hearing. Could it be possible? Someone wanted her!

That night was the Christmas pageant for the parents and neighbors on Montgomery Street. The neighbors had to look twice. Were those some of the Montgomery Street Gang as shepherds and wise men? *A Christmas miracle*, many of them thought.

Outside the center that night, the snow continued to fall, and the wind was blowing the snow into drifts. But inside the center, for all the center kids, the Montgomery Street Gang, Maria, and everyone else, it was the best Christmas ever!

About the Illustrator

*J*ames R. Chrisfield is a Syracuse native and a retired history teacher.

About the Author

Emily Ramsdell serves with the ministry of Child Evangelism Fellowship. She and her husband, Jim, reside in Syracuse, New York.